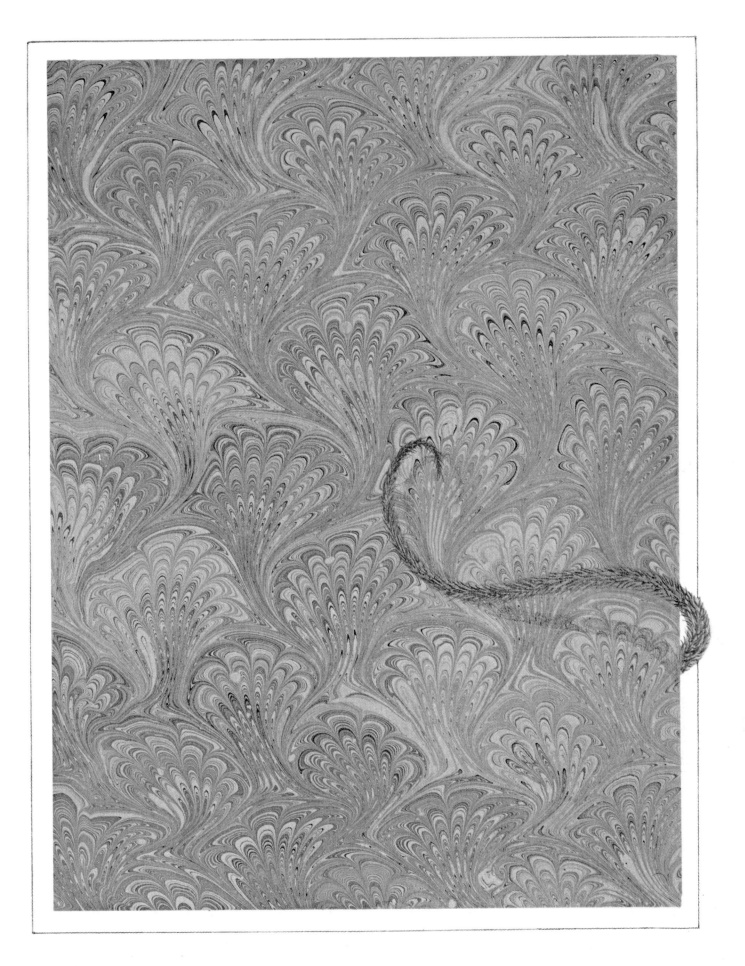

THE DEVIL

WITH THE

THREE GOLDEN HAIRS

The Devil
with the
Three Golden Hairs

A TALE FROM THE BROTHERS GRIMM
RETOLD AND ILLUSTRATED BY NONNY HOGROGIAN

ALFRED A. KNOPF · NEW YORK

THIS IS A BORZOI BOOK
PUBLISHED BY ALFRED A. KNOPF, INC.

Copyright © 1983 by Nonny H. Kherdian
All rights reserved under International and Pan-American Copyright Conventions.
Published in the United States by Alfred A. Knopf, Inc., New York,
and simultaneously in Canada by Random House of Canada Limited, Toronto.
Distributed by Random House, Inc., New York.
2   4   6   8   0   9   7   5   3   1
Manufactured in the United States of America
First Edition

Library of Congress Cataloging in Publication Data
Hogrogian, Nonny. The devil with the three golden hairs.
Summary: A boy born to a poor couple receives the hand of the king's daughter
in marriage, but in order to keep his bride, the boy must bring
the king three golden hairs from the head of the devil.
[1. Fairy tales. 2. Folklore—Germany]   I. Teufel mit den drei goldenen Haaren. English.
II. Title.   PZ8.H687De 1982   398.2'1'0943   82-12735
ISBN 0-394-85560-4   ISBN 0-394-95560-9 (lib. bdg.)

FOR T.W.

nce upon a time a boy with a caul was born to a poor couple. They were more than usually happy at his birth because they knew the caul was a certain sign that he would be very lucky. In fact, it was foretold that in his fourteenth year the boy would marry the king's daughter.

The king, who had a wicked heart and was disturbed by what he heard, went quickly to the parents and offered much gold in exchange for their son. At first the couple refused, but finally they said, "He is a luck-child and all must go well with him. Perhaps this was meant to be." And they consented to give up their infant.

The king laid the child in a box and rode on until he came to a deep river. He threw the box into the river and went on his way, saying, "I no longer have to worry about an unsuitable bridegroom for my daughter."

The box did not sink but floated along in the water until at last it came to shore by an old mill. The miller, who was fortunately standing nearby, pulled the box out of the river, hoping to find a treasure. When he opened the box, he saw the beautiful infant smiling up at him.

He took him home to his wife, saying, "God has sent him to us." And from that day on they cared for him as their own.

Years passed and one day the king stopped at the mill for shelter and was attended to by the youth. The king asked the miller if the boy was his. The miller began to tell him the story, and as he did the king realized it was the luck-child, and he said to the couple, "Good people, I would like the boy to take a letter to the queen, and I will give him two pieces of gold for his trouble."

"As my lord the king commands," they replied.

The king quickly wrote a letter, which said, "*As soon as the boy arrives with this letter, have him killed and buried, and have it done before I return.*"

The boy set out on his journey, but he lost his way in a storm. By nightfall he found himself walking toward a small cottage in a great forest. An old woman answered his knock.

"Why do you come here?" she asked. "What do you want?"

"I am carrying a letter to the queen," replied the boy, "but I lost my way in the storm, and I wish to spend the night here."

"Poor boy," she said. "You have come to a den of thieves, and when they return, they will kill you."

"Let them come," he said. "I am not afraid. I am too tired to go on." And he stretched himself upon a bench and went to sleep. When the robbers returned home, they were shocked to see the boy lying there.

"This poor youth was lost in the storm," said the old woman, "and I took him in out of compassion. He is carrying a letter to the queen."

The robbers seized the letter and read it, and they, too, felt compassion for him. They tore up the letter and replaced it with another, which stated that on his arrival he was to be married to the princess. The youth slept quietly through the night, and when he awoke, they gave him the letter and fed him and led him to the correct path.

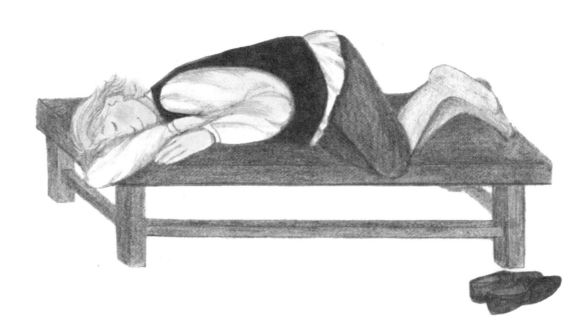

When the queen received the youth, she did exactly as the letter commanded. A wonderful marriage feast was prepared, and the princess was given in marriage to the boy. The princess and the luck-child lived happily until the king returned and found the prophecy fulfilled, in spite of his efforts.

He was in a rage when he saw the boy. "I will not allow it to be so easy for you," he exclaimed. "If you will have my daughter, first you must obtain for me three golden hairs from the head of the devil."

"I don't fear the devil," replied the youth. "I will go at once to fetch his three golden hairs and win back my bride," and he left the palace grounds.

The road led him by a large city. A watchman guarded the gate and asked him what his trade was and what he knew.

"I know everything," replied the boy.

"Then you can do us a kindness," said the watchman. "Tell us why the fountain in our marketplace, from which wine used to flow, will not even produce water now."

"I will tell you," answered the boy, "but you must wait until I return."

As he continued on his way he came to another city. Again there was a guard who asked him his trade and what he knew.

The boy replied, "I know everything."

"Then you can do us a favor and tell us why our tree, which once bore apples of gold, now does not even have any leaves."

"I will tell you, but you must wait until I return."

The boy continued on his way until he came to a huge lake. On the other side the devil made his home. As the ferryman rowed him across the lake, he asked the youth what his trade was and what he knew.

"I know everything," he replied.

"Then you can do me a kindness and tell me why I am obliged to row back and forth forever and ever."

"I will tell you," said the boy, "but you must wait until I return."

Soon after he reached the other shore, the boy found the devil's kingdom. The devil's old grandmother let him into the dark and gloomy place and asked him what he wanted.

"I want three golden hairs from the devil's head, in order to have my bride back," he said.

"That is a bold request," said the old woman. "If he comes home and finds you here, it will go bad for you. But if you wish, you can stay and I will try to help you."

So she turned him into an ant and told him to crawl into the gathers of her gown, where he would be well hidden.

The boy did as she bid him, and then he said, "There are three things I need to know. There is a fountain not far away from which wine used to flow. Why is it that now it will not even give a drop of water? And why a tree, which used to bear golden apples, now no longer has any leaves? And why the ferryman must row back and forth forever, never to be released?"

"Your questions are difficult," said the old woman, "but if you will pay close attention to what the devil says when I pluck the golden hairs, you will have your answers."

The devil soon returned, and the moment he entered the door, he said, "I smell the flesh of man." He looked in every corner but found nothing.

His grandmother began to scold him. "Why, I have just cleaned the house and put everything in its proper place, and now you are pulling it apart again. You are always having a man's flesh in your nose. Sit down and eat your supper."

The devil ate so much supper that he wore himself out, and his grandmother took his head in her lap and began to stroke his forehead. He blinked and yawned and finally fell asleep. Then she plucked the first golden hair and laid it down beside her.

The devil jumped and cried, "What are you doing, old woman?"

"Oh, I had a very bad dream, so I plucked one of your hairs," answered the old woman. "I dreamed there was a fountain in a marketplace from which wine used to flow, but it dried up and it will not give even a drop of water. What do you think is the matter with it?"

The devil rubbed his head before answering. "A toad is sitting under a stone in the spring," he replied, "and if he is killed, the wine will flow as before."

The old woman stroked his head again until he began to snore, and then—pluck!—she pulled the second golden hair from his head.

The devil jumped again and hollered as before, "What are you doing?"

"Don't be angry," his grandmother said. "It happened from my bad dream."

"What did you dream this time?" he shouted.

"I dreamed of the most beautiful tree, which grew in the center of a certain royal city, and it bore apples of pure gold. Now it no longer has even a leaf upon it. How can this be?"

"I can tell you why," the devil answered. "There is a mouse gnawing at the roots of the tree, and if he is killed, the tree will once again bear apples of gold. But if he isn't killed, he will keep gnawing at the roots until the tree dies completely. Now don't disturb me again, or I will beat you, old woman."

But the old woman simply rocked him to sleep again and plucked the third golden hair. He jumped in a fury this time, but she looked at him innocently and said, "Who can help bad dreams?"

"Well," the devil said after he had calmed down, "you may as well tell me about it now that I am wide awake."

"Oh, I dreamed of our poor ferryman who is obliged to row back and forth, never to be released. Why is he made to suffer so?"

"You foolish old woman," said the devil. "The only way he can be released is to give the oar into the hand of another who wants to go across. Then the other person will be obliged to go forward and back and the ferryman will be free."

The old woman had plucked the three golden hairs and had received the answers to the questions, so she soothed the devil back to sleep, and he snored until daybreak.

As soon as he left in the morning, the old woman helped the ant out of the folds of her gown and restored him to his human form. Then she presented the boy with the three golden hairs from the head of the devil.

He thanked the old woman for her assistance and assured her that he remembered the devil's answers, and he began his journey home.

When he saw the ferryman, he said, "Row me across and then I will give you the answer you seek." As soon as they reached the other side and he set his feet on land, he said, "When the next man comes this way and wants you to take him across, put the oar in his hand."

The boy continued his journey home and came to the city with the barren tree. The guard was waiting for his answer.

"Kill the mouse that gnaws at the roots of the tree and it will soon bear golden apples again."

The guard gave the order, and before long the tree was in full bloom again. The boy was given two donkeys laden with gold.

He went on his way until he came to the city of the dry fountain. The watchman was waiting for him.

"Under a stone in the spring there sits a toad. You must uncover and kill him, and then the wine will flow as it did before."

The order was given, and soon the wine began to flow as before. Again the boy was rewarded with two donkeys laden with gold.

When he arrived home, his bride was overjoyed. He gave the king the three golden hairs from the devil's head, but when the king saw the four donkeys laden with gold, his eyes began to glitter.

"You have earned the right to have my daughter," he said. "But tell me, my son, where did you find all this gold?"

"I was ferried across a river," the boy said, "where the shore was covered with it, like sand at the sea."

The greedy king said, "I would like to gather some gold too."

"Gather as much as you like," said the boy. "There is a ferryman who will row you across the river. You can fill your sack on the other side."

The king set out immediately, and before long he came to the river. The ferryman was waiting and told the king to step into his boat. As soon as he did, the ferryman put the oar into the hand of the king and jumped onto the shore to freedom.

So the king was obliged to take the ferryman's place, and there he still rows, forever, back and forth, back and forth, for no one has come to take his place.

The youth, together with his bride, lived well and reigned well, for he who is not afraid can even take the hairs from the devil's head and conquer the kingdom.

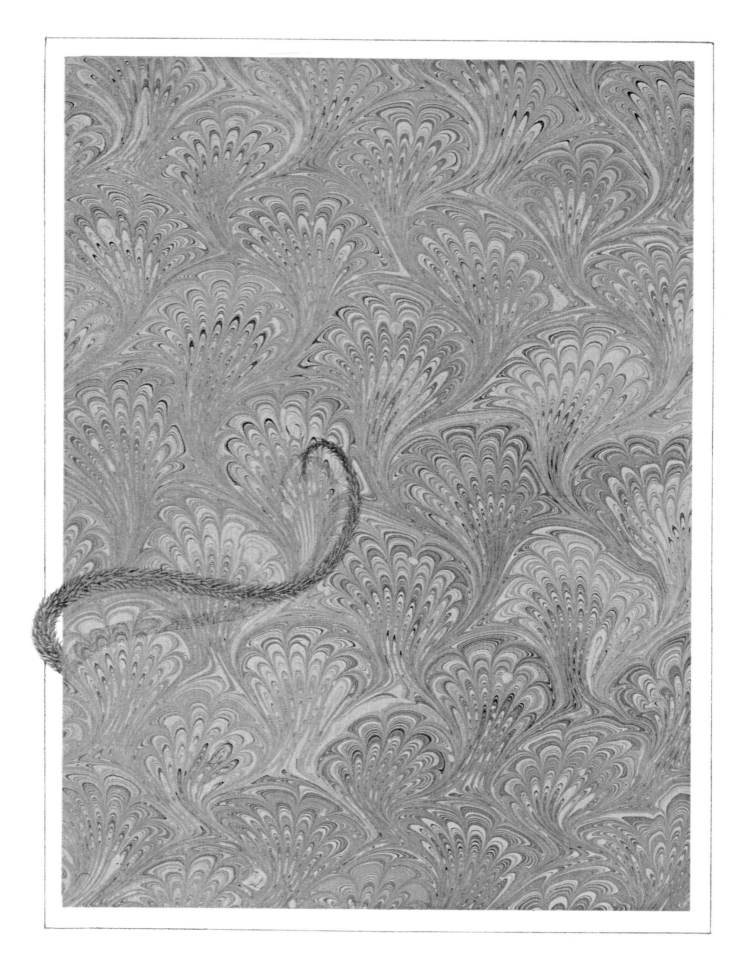